WORLD WAR I TALES

TERRY DEARY

THE WAR GAME

Illustrated by James de la Rue

A & C BLACK
AN IMPRINT OF BLOOMSBURY
LONDON NEW DELHI   NEW YORK   SYDNEY

Chapter 1
Soft, short shirts

Northern France – December 1914

Albert Watson sang at the top of his voice as he marched along the crumbling roads of France. The other soldiers liked to sing '*It's a long way to Tipperary*'. But Albert didn't even know where Tipperary was. He didn't care if it was a long way or a short way to Tipperary.

They had sung themselves silly with, '*Forward Joe Soap's army, marching without fear.*' He knew that 'Joe Soap' meant 'dope', a dummy, and he didn't like to think he was in an army of dopes.

Albert hated the song,
'I don't want to be a soldier,
I don't want to go to war,
I'd rather stay at home,
Around the streets to roam.'

It just wasn't true that he'd 'rather stay at home'... though he did miss home on the coldest nights. And of course he missed his mum's cooking when he chewed on the stew at the army canteen. Even the plum and apple jam was tough.

No, Albert could bear the homesickness. He was proud to be on his way to fight the Germans. And he was happy now the troop were singing his favourite marching song.

He chanted the words to the beat of a thousand boots.

'Yes, Sister Susie's sewing shirts for soldiers,
Such skill at sewing shirts my shy young
    sister Susie shows,
Some soldiers send epistles, say they'd
    sooner sleep on thistles,
Than the saucy, soft, short shirts for
    soldiers sister Susie sews.'

He could always manage the tongue-twisting words while his mates tangled their tonsils. He remembered the time Charlie Embleton tried to sing, 'soft, short shirts' and managed to spit out his false teeth. They fell in the mud and he had to scramble to collect them before the man behind stepped on them. Charlie knew he'd never get new teeth in the battlefields of France and Flanders.

As Charlie had stooped to collect the teeth, the man behind had fallen over him and twenty troopers ended up in a heap on the rutted road. The sergeant was furious. Mind you, it didn't take much to make the sergeant's moustache bristle, his face turn red and his throat roar like Barney's bull.

The sergeant punished Charlie by placing him on guard duty from midnight till sunrise at eight the next morning. Charlie kept himself happy by singing rude songs about sergeants.

'If the sergeant steals your rum, never
    mind;
For he's just a drunken sot,
Let him have the ruddy lot,
If the sergeant steals your rum, never
    mind.'

Albert liked old Charlie. Albert's dad had died in a coal-mine when Albert was nine. Charlie was a bit like a dad to him, now they were so far from home.

When the Sister Susie song had finished Albert made sure the sergeant wasn't looking, and turned to Charlie, marching by his side.

'I didn't hear you singing *soft, short shirts*, Charlie,' the young man teased.

Charlie glared at him and pointed to the sharp blade on his belt.

'See this bayonet, sonny boy?

'Yes, Charlie.'

'Then shut up or I'll stick it in your backside.'

'Shut up about what?' Albert asked.

'About me singing *soft, short shirts...*' Charlie tried to say.

But before he could finish Charlie's teeth
had flown over Albert's head and into the
ditch at the side of the road.

Chapter 2
Pawns and practice

The first days in France were spent training. Albert spent a lot of time having his ears battered by the Barney's-bull bellow of the big, bruising bully of a sergeant. The lad ran up and down the camp training ground. His bayonet was fixed to the barrel of his gun as the troop took it in turns to stab at straw-stuffed dummies.

'Stick it in as far as it will go... twist it... pull it out,' Sergeant Carter shouted.

As they rested with a tin mug of bitter tea, Albert turned to Charlie. 'You were in the last war, in South Africa.'

Charlie's back went straight. 'I was. Out in the heat of South Africa. Not like this freezing mud. We was fighting for old Queen Victoria in them days. Till she died, of course. Then we was fighting for King Edward.'

'But did you stick your bayonet into many men?' Albert pressed. 'I mean... I can stick it in a dummy. But a real man, that's different.'

Charlie chewed on a piece of tobacco. 'No, son. These days you can't go charging at your enemy with bayonets. Not even back in Queen Victoria's day. I never stabbed anyone. They shoot you before you get to fifty yards. With the machine guns them Germans have, they'd wipe us all out before we got over their barbed wire. No, son, bayonets aren't a lot of use in this war.'

Albert nodded. 'So why are we practising with them?'

'Because that's what the officers want. Have you ever played chess?'

'You want to play chess?' asked Albert. 'Now?'

Charlie sighed. 'I'm just saying, do you know what chess is?'

'Of course I do, Charlie. I'm not daft. I went to school till I was thirteen.'

'You move your men around a chess board, right? Well, our General French has a big board like that. He has two armies

– the First and Second Armies. And our friends in France and so on have their own armies. And the generals move us around like pawns on a chess board, see?'

'And the Germans do the same?'
'Exactly.' Charlie nodded.
Albert stamped his feet to warm them on the cold, hard earth of the parade

ground. Everything was grey and brown. The sky was the colour of a coal-miner's bath water but not so warm. There was a steady rumble like thunder as the big guns on each side sent their shells down like steel hailstones.

'When do we join this game then, Charlie?' he asked.

Charlie looked up at the sky where the flashes from the guns lit the low clouds. 'We're not far from the fighting, son. We'll be there this time next week.'

Albert nodded slowly. 'That's Christmas in the trenches for us, then?'

Charlie blew out his cheeks. 'Christmas? In a war Christmas Day is the same as any other day.'

But for once Charlie Embleton was wrong.

Chapter 3
Postcards and plans

Captain Forsythe called the troops onto the parade ground the next day. 'Stand easy men,' he began. The soldiers relaxed but looked grim. They knew what was coming.

'Tomorrow you move ten miles forward. You men will be the reserve line. The chaps at the front in the trenches are ready for a break. The day after tomorrow you will take their place. Half of you will be the front line and the other half the rear line. You'll swap over every twelve hours.'

Captain Forsythe was young – maybe just twenty years old – and had the shining pink face of a schoolboy.

'You may write postcards home tonight,' he said.

'That'll be in case we don't come back,' Charlie muttered out of the side of his mouth.

'But you must not say where you are. A German spy may read your message and discover our plans.' The young officer tried to look like a stern school prefect. 'This is top secret stuff. Any questions?'

Albert's hand shot in the air as if he were in the classroom. 'Please sir,' he said.

'Yes?'

'Will we be attacking with bayonets or rifles or machine guns?'

Captain Forsythe looked unsure. 'I don't think you'll be attacking at all.'

'So why are we going?' another soldier asked.

'Because those are our orders,' the officer said, blushing a little.

'Yes, sir,' Charlie put in, 'but I think he means, *why* do we have those orders?'

Captain Forsythe cleared his throat.

'The Germans are the attackers. We have dug lines of trenches, hundreds of miles of them. The trenches are filled with British and French troops like us. Our job is to stop them getting any further. If we aren't there then the Germans will take over the whole of France. Their next stop would be Britain. Your children will be speaking German if you men don't do your jobs.'

'So we defend?' Charlie said.

'Unless orders come for us to attack,' Captain Forsythe said.

He gave a shrug. 'For now, defend. Stay in your trench. If you see a German, shoot him.'

'If he doesn't shoot us first,' someone muttered and the men laughed.

'Well, keep your heads down,' the Captain said.

'Ah,' Charlie said, 'but if we keep our heads down, we won't be able to see the enemy. They could run across from their trenches and jump into ours. How can we shoot the Germans if we can't stick our heads up and look for them?'

'Look out from time to time,' Captain Forsythe shouted, his pink face now turning red. 'Lift your eyes over the top.'

'What about if the German shoots me in the eye?' The men laughed louder.

Captain Forsythe carried a short wooden stick. He rapped it against his leg, then pointed it at Charlie Embleton. 'Sergeant Carter.'

'Yes, sir?' the sergeant said smartly.

'Put that man on a charge. Have him cleaning the toilets from now until we march to the trenches.'

The sergeant's grin split his face and showed his yellow, tobacco-stained teeth. 'It'll be a pleasure, sir.'

Charlie Embleton sighed and began to sing, as softly as sister Susie's shirts, '*If the sergeant steals your rum, never mind.*'

Chapter 4
Christmas comforts

A wind blew hard across the North Sea. The wind didn't stop at Belgium. It brought flecks of snow to the trenches of northern France.

Albert wore mittens with no fingers. He rested his rifle against the hard-frozen wall of the trench and blew on his hands. 'It's cold,' he said and shuddered.

'Good thing too,' Charlie Embleton said.

'My toes don't think it's good,' the young soldier argued.

'If the ground wasn't frozen then you'd be standing in mud. And mud's worse than ice. You can wrap up against the cold, but mud... what does mud do?'

'I don't know. What does mud do?' Albert asked.

'It seeps through every seam of your uniform. You get wet as well as cold, and it takes a lot longer to warm up.'

'So cold is good, eh?'

'Cold is good. And remember, it's as cold for Jerry as it is for us.'

Albert slowly raised his head above the edge of the trench and looked through the rows of barbed wire to the German trenches. 'Is that why they're quiet?' he asked.

'It is.' Charlie nodded. 'The Germans don't have muddy little holes in the ground like us. They have proper underground shelters, cosy and warm. You'll see when we start attacking in the springtime. We'll capture one and be snug as rabbits in a burrow.'

'We have to wait till spring to attack?' Albert sighed. 'I've been in the army six months now and I've never fired a bullet at an enemy.'

'You'll see plenty of bullets soon enough. It's the one you don't see that's the dangerous one. That'll be the one that hits you if you don't keep your head down.'

Albert ducked back down under the cover of the trench. He stamped his feet and blew on his hands again. 'They said this war would be over by Christmas. They say that back home a million men have rushed to join the British Army. They're all worried that the war will finish before they get here!'

Albert shivered inside his khaki uniform. It fitted badly: the jacket was too baggy and let in draughts around the neck and sleeves; tight khaki bandages were wrapped round his legs to keep out mud, but they made those legs look thin enough to snap. A German would see those matchstick legs marching towards him and die laughing. The young man's large boots and frost-red nose made him look like a sad, brown clown.

He looked down at Charlie. The older man had cropped hair that showed grey where he'd pushed his helmet back. Charlie sat at the entrance to a crude cave dug into the frozen soil. He was trying to boil a kettle over a small fire in a biscuit tin.

'Tell you what, Albert,' he said, wiping a dew-drop off the end of his battered nose. 'We'll try to keep this war going a bit longer, shall we? Just to give you a bit of excitement?'

'You can,' Albert said. 'I'm due a bit of leave in the New Year. I want to get back home and see my mum! I've never had a Christmas away from home before.'

'When you've been in the army as long as I have...' Charlie said solemnly.

'Here we go,' Albert muttered into his cupped hands as he breathed on them for warmth. 'The Boer War. Next you'll be telling me you fought for Britain when Julius Caesar invaded.'

'When you've been in the army as long as I have, you'll forget what a Christmas at home is like!' Charlie declared.

'Well, Christmas at home is warmer than it is here, I can tell you,' the younger man sniffed.

'I told you, you don't want it any warmer, son! If it wasn't for the cold we'd be over our ankles in mud.'

'You always look on the bright side, don't you, Charlie?'

'You have to, son. It could be worse. We could have had orders to attack the German trenches today. Some German sniper could have sent you a little present from the end of his rifle. You could be lying out there in No Man's Land with a bullet in your brain,' the older man told him. 'Though you'd probably be safe, come to think of it. Your brain being such a small target and all.'

'Ha ha. Very funny, Charlie.'

'And you've got your chocolate and your tobacco and your Christmas card from the king and queen, haven't you? Your Christmas comforts.'

Ah, yes, Albert thought. The best thing that had happened to him since he joined the army. Maybe the best thing that had happened in his life.

Chapter 5
Silver and brass

Albert Watson slid a hand into the pocket of his great coat. The card was there. A Christmas card. The most amazing Christmas card he'd ever had.

It was a card from the king himself. It made him proud to have that message, even if it was just a print of His Majesty's handwriting. Albert didn't need to read it because he knew the words by heart. But he stole a look at it anyway.

'May God protect you and bring you home safe.'

He'd read the words a hundred times until it was too dark to read them any

more. 'Bring you home safe,' he thought. Those four words were the ones that made him just a little homesick.

'It's quiet, isn't it?' he said suddenly. 'Do you reckon Jerry's gone home for Christmas? I haven't heard a shot for hours.'

The thunder of the guns had faded with the setting sun. There was no use firing when you couldn't see what your shells were hitting.

Charlie was leaning forward, his putty-coloured face pale and frozen in the faint light of a half moon. He stared across the wasteland – shattered earth with ice-filled pits where a shell had landed. The mud was silver in the light and looked like the surface of the moon itself. No Man's Land, they called it.

Charlie's hand slid down and wrapped itself round the rifle that lay there. 'What's that noise?' he whispered.

Albert raised his head and looked across No Man's Land towards the German trenches. Charlie jumped forward and dragged the young man roughly down. 'You want to get your head blown off, young Albert?' he hissed. 'There's marksmen just waiting for idiots like you to look over the top! Snipers. The best shots in the German army.'

'You hurt my elbow!' Albert complained.

'Shush! Listen!'

The two men huddled on the frozen floor of the trench and strained their ears.

'It's a band!' the young soldier breathed. 'It's a blooming brass band!'

'Maybe they're going to attack us with trombones.' Charlie chuckled.

'No! They're playing *Silent Night*!'

'A bit risky, that.'

'Why?'

'It's giving away their position,' the older man explained.

'But it's lovely,' Albert said. His throat was tight and his eyes pricked with tears.

There was a faint whistle over the top of the music. The men clutched their heads and shrunk down, not knowing where the shell would land. It grew louder till it was a wail that drowned the music and it ended with a sudden crash that came from the far side of No Man's Land.

'I told you,' Charlie said. 'One of our gunners isn't in the Christmas spirit. He missed their trenches by a long way. He was closer to us than the Germans.'

'Our gunners wouldn't shell their own men.' Albert gave a nervous laugh.

'It's happened before,' Charlie said grimly.

The men rose to their feet and peered over the rim of their trench. A spiral of blue smoke climbed into the sky as echoes of the explosion faded into the night.

'What did our gunners do that for?' Albert groaned. 'That was nice music, that was!'

'That'll be the generals for you.'

'Don't they know it's Christmas?'

'Christmas? They can't even spell the word.'

Albert nodded sadly. 'I had the same trouble spelling when I was at school.'

A ghostly silence fell over the silver scene again.

Chapter 6

Salutes and songs

The men turned back to their tea. It tasted terrible but it warmed them.

Captain Forsythe crunched through the iced mud of the trench and asked, 'Everything all right, Corporal Embleton?'

Charlie scrambled to his feet, snapped a salute and straightened his back. 'Yes, sir.'

'Shouldn't one of you be looking out? There could be Germans heading this way right at this moment!'

'Sir!' Charlie said and turned to look over the rim. 'Cor, stone the crows!' he gasped. 'Look at that!'

Albert and the officer joined him and looked across about a hundred paces. In the still evening air, about a hundred candles were flickering on a dozen fir trees that the Germans had raised above the trenches and planted in their half of No Man's Land.

Around each tree there were groups of five to ten German soldiers, sitting and talking. In the still evening air their voices drifted across.

Albert called, 'Merry Christmas, Fritz!'

There was a short pause. Then a German voice replied, 'Merry Christmas, Tommy!'

'My name's Albert!' the young man shouted.

'Come here!' the German called. 'We meet. We shake hands! You don't shoot – we don't shoot!'

Albert began to scramble over the top but Captain Forsythe grabbed his belt and pulled him back.

'It could be a trick.'

'I never thought of that, sir.'

'It's a risk you should not take.'

'No, sir.'

The German called again. 'It is Christmas! We shake hands!'

The young officer straightened his back. 'I'll go and see what they want. If they shoot me, kill every German you can see. Cover me with your rifles.'

'Yes, sir.'

Captain Forsythe climbed into No Man's Land. A German searchlight flooded the frozen desert of mud and made the officer shield his eyes. He slowly unbuckled his pistol belt and let it fall to the ground. British troops in the trenches to his right and left raised their heads to watch.

One German stood up and walked out to meet him. The whole world seemed to hold its breath and even the face of the man in the moon froze.

When the German officer met Captain Forsythe he saluted smartly. The young English soldier with the face of a startled schoolboy returned the salute. Then he stretched out a hand and the German grasped it.

As they shook hands, a cheer broke out from the British trenches. It was answered by a cheer from the enemy.

The German soldiers began singing *Silent Night* while the two men in the middle seemed to be having a long and friendly chat. When the carol was finished there was a silence in the night and a British soldier cried, 'Can't you sing *It's a long way to Tipperary?*'

'We will sing it for you, Tommy!' a German replied and the night was filled with the curious sound of German troops roaring out a British marching song.

One by one the British soldiers joined in. Albert forgot that he didn't like the song. He could hardly sing for laughing.

Chapter 7

Pot-holed pitch

As the German soldiers struggled to sing *God Save the King*, Captain Forsythe headed back to the British side and soldiers gathered round him. The officer was not much older than Private Albert Watson. His eyes were sparkling and his pale cheeks had pink spots in them.

'I've spoken to their commander and agreed that we will have a truce for forty-eight hours. Neither side will fire till after Boxing Day.'

The men cheered and Albert turned to Charlie Embleton. 'That's good news, Charlie.'

The older man shook his head. 'Never seen anything like it in twenty years. It never happened in the Boer War. Anyone who tried it would have been shot.'

'By the Boers?'

'No, by the British, you dummy! They can't have people going round making friends with the enemy.'

'Why not?'

'Because, young feller, it would put us all out of a job.' Charlie grinned. Then the grin faded. 'Young Captain Forsythe is taking a bit of a chance, talking to the enemy like that. The generals won't like it, you'll see.'

'The generals? They're probably roasting a goose and steaming their Christmas puddings, miles away in a big warm house. What do they care?' Albert asked.

'We'll see.' Charlie shrugged. 'We'll see.'

As Christmas Eve slipped into Christmas morning the singing began to fade. Charlie and Albert went to the rear trenches for some sleep and returned the next morning.

Albert looked carefully over the top of the trench and saw a group of twenty Germans climb out with a football. They

kicked it over the uneven ground and
passed it to one another.

'I was a good footballer,' Albert said.

'What? With legs like yours?' Charlie
scoffed. 'Never!'

'I was! I'll bet I could teach those
Germans a trick or two.'

'Go on, then.'

'You what?'

Charlie climbed up to No Man's Land and shouted across to the enemy, 'Albert Watson here's a star footballer. He says he could beat you with one foot tied behind his back!'

The Germans laughed. 'We are best football players in world!'

Other sentries heard the cry and roared back, 'Rubbish!' More British soldiers climbed up onto the crackling mud, and someone said, 'Eleven-a-side! Let's see how good you are!'

The Germans gathered into a group to choose their best eleven while the British troops did the same. Albert stood shyly in the group until Sergeant Carter pointed to him. 'Best right-winger in the town until he joined up.'

No one argued and Albert found himself stripping off his jacket and running onto

the roughest pot-holed football pitch the
world had ever seen. A German officer
had a whistle and acted as referee and
timekeeper.

He blew and the match was under way.

Chapter 7
Shots and sweat

For an hour there was no war.

There was plenty of fight, though. Albert found that every time he ran forward with the ball he was kicked and tripped by a short, heavy German with a red face and thin, fair hair.

After one tackle Albert was sure his ankle was broken. Only his heavy army boots saved him.

His opponent booted the ball up the field, where the tall German officer hit it with a glancing header into the goal that was formed by rifles stuck in the hard earth.

Charlie stood on the side-lines telling
Albert how to play. 'You can't dribble on
this ground. You keep losing the ball. One
touch then boot it up for Sergeant Carter
to head.'

Albert was annoyed. 'Could you do
better?' he asked.

'I could,' Charlie said. 'But I might lose
me teeth.'

The longer the game went on, the slower the heavy German became. Albert was sweating in his woollen shirt in spite of the icy air. But his legs were as strong and quick as ever.

'Five minutes to go!' the referee cried.

Captain Forsythe collected the ball from his goalkeeper and passed it to Sergeant Carter. A German ran at the sergeant but he bounced off the solid British shoulder.

Sergeant Carter looked up and spotted Albert alone on the right wing. He kicked the ball towards him.

The ball bounced and bobbled to Albert. He turned and saw his enemy charging towards him.

The German's boots skidded over the earth in a slide that would break Albert's skinny legs. But Albert pushed the ball forward, jumped over the lunging German legs and raced towards the goal.

He raised his boot and looked to shoot to the goalkeeper's right.

The goalkeeper dived to his right too soon. Albert had sold him a dummy. He coolly slid the ball to the man's left and between the rifle-goalposts.

The British soldiers cheered till their throats were raw and Albert had never felt so proud in his life.

When the final whistle blew a few minutes later he was carried off the pitch on the shoulders of the happy British troops. The other players were shaking hands with their opponents.

The British team dropped Albert at Charlie's feet.

'Lucky shot,' Charlie said with a sniff. Albert just grinned.

The young man jogged back to the pitch. Sergeant Carter was happy. Albert had never seen him look so pleased. 'Well played, Watson. Cracking goal.'

'Thank you, sir. Lovely pass from you.'

'Not bad. We could have won with a bit more luck.'

Albert shook his head slowly. For the first time in his life, he argued with the sergeant. 'A draw was the best result, sir. It's Christmas.'

Sergeant Carter wrapped an arm around his shoulder. 'Aye, you're probably right. Happy Christmas, lad.'

As the sergeant walked away another figure walked towards Albert. The heavy, red-faced German scowled at him. Suddenly he stuck out a fat arm. 'Shake hand, Englishman. Good played.'

'Good played, Fritz.' Albert grinned.

The German allowed himself a small smile. It made him look much younger. Younger even than Albert. 'Not Fritz. Hans. My name Hans.'

'My name Albert. Good played, Hans.'

'Good played, Albert.'

They kept the handshake firm as they looked into one another's eyes for half a minute or more. 'Good shoot,' Hans said.

'Thanks,' Albert replied and felt himself blushing.

Suddenly the German's eyes turned glassy and his face bleak. 'Today shoot football. Tomorrow shoot guns.'

Albert's head dropped. 'Aye.'

When he looked up, Hans was marching back towards his trench. 'Hans!' Albert cried.

The German stopped and turned.

'Good luck,' Albert said. He recited the words from his memory as if they were some magic charm. 'May God protect you and bring you home safe.'

Hans gave a brief nod. 'You too, Albert. You too.'

Chapter 7
Truce trouble

As Albert and Charlie sat in the still evening air drinking foul-tasting tea, Sergeant Carter appeared in the trench. 'Right, you lot. On parade at base camp. The other half of the troop will take your place.'

The soldiers bustled to collect their kit-bags and weapons and obey.

'He looked serious,' Albert said. The memory of the Sergeant's warm arm around his shoulder that morning seemed like a dream.

'It means trouble,' Charlie said.

When they arrived on the parade ground Captain Forsythe was waiting for them. 'Stand at ease,' he cried, his thin voice lost in the moon-grey clouds. 'Now. General French has heard stories of soldiers having truces with their German enemies.'

'That's a disgrace,' Sergeant Carter barked.

'There are even stories of British soldiers playing football with the enemy.'

'I can't believe that, sir,' Carter snapped.

'I told the general that my men would never do such a thing. That football match never happened. If any man saw someone playing football with the enemy he must step forward now.'

No one moved. At last Charlie Embleton stepped forward.

'Excuse me, sir, but I did hear about that football game that never happened. I heard that a captain and a sergeant played for the British team.'

Captain Forsythe turned to Sergeant Carter. 'Have you ever heard such nonsense, Sergeant?'

'Never, sir.'

The captain nodded. 'Do you have any toilets that need cleaning, sergeant?'

'A couple of hundred, sir.' The officers looked at Charlie.

Captain Forsythe spoke. 'So, Embleton. What did you hear about this football match?'

Charlie sucked on his false teeth. 'I heard it never happened, sir.'

The Captain smiled. 'Correct. Troop dismiss. And get a good night's sleep.' Then he said quietly, so that only Albert's sharp ears heard the slow sad words, 'Tomorrow we go to war.'

Epilogue

A Christmas truce, like the one in 1914, had been seen in many other wars. At first the British troops thought the German Christmas trees were a trick and shot them down. The Germans put them back up and the British stopped firing.

There were many reports of football matches between the enemies. Some were organised and others were just friendly kick-abouts with a hundred men joining in.

Some truces went on until New Year's Day but most ended after Boxing Day. In one part of the trenches the British politely told the Germans, 'We will start shooting again at nine o'clock.' The Germans called back, 'Then we'll come over to your trenches – we'll be safer!' Many of the men found it hard to start fighting again. When their officers gave the order to shoot, the soldiers replied, 'We can't – they are good fellows and we can't.'

The officers replied, 'If you don't start firing then we will – and it won't be at the Germans.'

The German troops had the same problem. For several days the British and Germans fired at one another without trying to hit. A soldier wrote, 'We spent that day and the next wasting ammunition in trying to shoot the stars from the sky.'

The generals on both sides were furious when they heard about the Christmas truce. As the First World War grew more bitter, a Christmas truce like 1914 was never seen again.

TERRY DEARY'S
VICTORIAN TALES

The Fabulous Flyer

Terror on the Train

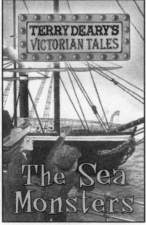

The Sea Monsters

The Twisted Tunnels